W9-BXE-237

Words to Know Before You Read

changed

freezer

fridge

garden

hungry

invited

kitchen

returned

slippers

trouble

www.rourkeeducationalmedia.com

Edited by Precious McKenzie
Illustrated by Helen Poole
Art Direction and Page Layout by Renee Brady

Library of Congress PCN Data

Little Miss Midge / Colleen Hord
ISBN 978-1-61810-178-5 (hard cover) (alk. paper)
ISBN 978-1-61810-311-6 (soft cover)
Library of Congress Control Number: 2012936778

Rourke Educational Media
Printed in the United States of America,
North Mankato, Minnesota

rourkeeducationalmedia.com

customerservice@rourkeeducationalmedia.com • PO Box 643328 Vero Beach, Florida 32964

Little Miss Midge

By Colleen Hord

Illustrated by Helen Poole

Little Miss Midge had a busy day ahead of her. She made a list so she wouldn't forget what she needed to do.

Things To Do!
- Buy my poor dog a bone
- Feed the dog
- Sweep the floor
- Make the bed
- Have friends in for ice cream

4

The first thing Little Miss Midge did was go to the fridge, to get her poor dog a bone. But when she got there, her fridge was bare.

"Oh my!" cried Miss Midge. "There is nothing in the fridge! I must go to the store."

Things To Do!
• Buy my poor dog a bone
• Feed the dog
• Sweep the floor
• Make the bed
• Have friends in for ice cream

But before she went to the store, she changed her list.

Miss Midge went to the store to buy her poor dog a bone. When she got home, she found him digging in her garden.

"Oh my!" said Miss Midge. "I must clean this mess up. Come and get your bone, silly dog, and see if you can stay out of trouble."

But before she began, she changed the order of her list.

Things To Do!
- Replant the flowers
- Sweep the floor
- Make the bed
- Have friends in for ice cream

Miss Midge finished planting the flowers in her garden and went back into the kitchen.

There she found her poor dog sitting by the fridge. "Are you still hungry?" asked Miss Midge.

So Little Miss Midge went to the fridge to get her poor dog a bone, but when she got there, once again, the fridge was bare.

"Oh my!" said Miss Midge. "I must go to the store to buy my poor dog a bone. But first I must change my list."

Miss Midge changed her list once more.

Things To Do!
• Buy my poor dog a bone
• Feed the dog
  Sweep the floor
  Make the bed
• Have friends in for ice cream

When Miss Midge returned home, she found her dog chewing up her slippers. "Oh my!" said Miss Midge, "I must clean up this mess. Come and get your bone, silly dog, and stay out of trouble."

So, one more time, Miss Midge changed the order of her list.

Things To Do!
- Clean up slipper mess
- Sweep the floor
- Make the bed
- Have friends in for ice cream

Just then, the doorbell rang. "Who could that be?" asked Miss Midge.
Miss Midge opened the door. "We're here!" shouted her friends. "We are ready for ice cream."

She went to the fridge to get ice cream, but when she got there, the freezer was bare. "Oh my," laughed Miss Midge. "I guess I must change my list again." But this time, she only wrote one thing on her list.

Things To Do!
• Take dog and friends OUT for ice cream!

After Reading Activities

You and the Story...

Have you ever had chores to do but didn't get them done?

Have you ever had to take care of a pet?

What would you do if your friends came over and you weren't finished with your chores?

Words You Know Now...

Choose four words from the list below and write four sentences about something that happened in the story.

changed	invited
freezer	kitchen
fridge	returned
garden	slippers
hungry	trouble

You Could...Make a List That Miss Midge's Dog Might Have Written for the Day

- Write a sequenced list that shows what the dog's day was like in the story.

- What things might Miss Midge have done to make the dog change his list?

- How would the ending of the story change using the dog's list?

About the Author

Colleen Hord is an elementary school teacher. Her favorite part of her teaching day is Writer's Workshop. She enjoys kayaking, camping, walking on the beach, and reading in her hammock.

Ask The Author!
www.rem4students.com

About the Illustrator

Helen Poole lives in Liverpool, England, with her fiancé. Over the past ten years she has worked as a designer and illustrator on books, toys, and games for many stores and publishers worldwide. Her favorite part of illustrating is character development. She loves creating fun, whimsical worlds with bright, vibrant colors. She gets her inspiration from everyday life and has her sketchbook with her at all times as inspiration often strikes in the unlikeliest of places!